The Winter Cow

Based on True Events

Rebecca A. Maticic

To my handsome boys, Clayton and Mason.
Your father would be so proud of you.
You will always have all my love,
and remember that you are never alone!

~Mom

With special thanks to Michael Boswell and all of
my farm family for continuing to stand by me.

And to "Winter"
...thank you for coming into our lives!

~Becky

1

It was a brisk Christmas Eve morning when the boys heard the warning barks from Levi and Stetson outside in the field. They ran to the door and looked out through the morning snow to see what would cause the dogs to be so worried.

The horses were lined up along the fence line, ears pricked and eyes wide, sensing there was something out of the norm. The dogs' alerts were heard by Pumba, the spotted potbelly pig, and he grunted to the gentle dairy goat, Jazzie. Roger, the rooster, crowed and all the hens fluffed their feathers.

The boys could see something lying in the corn field near the crest of the hill. Wondering what it could be, they grabbed their jackets and boots and started out toward it.

As they approached, it looked like a deer, but white? *It couldn't be a white deer*, they thought, so slowly and quietly they moved forward.

A quiet "Moooo" escaped from the fragile little creature. "It's a cow! It's a baby cow!" the boys exclaimed.

Only a few hours old, it was cold, wet, and weak, and the cow's mother was nowhere in sight.

Taking their jackets off, the boys swiftly wrapped up the little bull calf and then carried him back to the farmhouse. They filled an old baby bottle with warmed milk, then found blankets in the closet and dragged them downstairs to the basement where they had placed the baby cow.

After suckling down the milk and snuggling up in the wool blankets, the calf finally stopped shivering. He licked the boys as if to say thank you, then fell fast asleep.

2

A few hours later, Mom was steadily working in the kitchen, getting ready for their big family Christmas dinner.

Hearing some rustling under the old wood floors, she rushed downstairs to find a mess of boxes, wrapping paper, and blankets. Unable to figure out how this mess came to be, she peered further into the pile of Christmas chaos. There in the middle, she found... two big, round, brown eyes that belonged to a fluffy white calf with Christmas bows stuck to his head.

"BOOYYSSS!" she screamed. "Why is there a *cow* in our house?"

The boys stumbled downstairs, falling over each other as they reached the bottom of the staircase where their mother stood square with her hands on her hips.

They exclaimed their story, one over top of the other, while she glared at them in disbelief.

As they pleaded to keep him, the little white wrapping-paper covered calf gazed up at her with a glimmer in his eye. Admiring her children's determination, and with sympathy for the poor little calf, she decided to allow them to keep the winter cow until he was strong enough to be on his own.

3

Later that afternoon, the boys attempted to feed the little white calf. He was not as frisky as he had been earlier. This lack of interest in his food alarmed them.

"He feels really warm. I think he has a fever," the older boy said.

So they sought out Mom for help in treating the calf. She contacted the local veterinarian, then drove to town to pick up medications.

While she was gone, the boys stayed wrapped up in the wool blankets with the ill little calf. His head lay resting on the older boy's lap as the younger boy softly stroked the cowlick of fur on his forehead.

"This reminds me of when Dad used to stroke my head when I was sick," the older boy said.

The baby cow lovingly gazed up at the smiles the boys shared, as they giggled and told stories of their father.

When Mom returned, she felt overwhelming warmth as she entered the farmhouse. In the basement, she found the boys holding the white calf and singing Christmas songs.

Hiding her concerns for the cow behind a smile, she demonstrated to the boys how to medicate the calf and take his temperature.

Still worried, the boys wanted to bring the calf upstairs so they could closely monitor him. "Can we, Mom?"

With a soft sigh and a tug at her heart, she lovingly agreed.

There lying by the Christmas tree, with the colored lights shining on the new Christmas cow, Mom shook her head with half of a smile. She saw a twinkle in the boys' eyes that she hadn't seen since their dad had been gone.

4

Santa was expected to arrive that evening and the boys' excitement just couldn't be contained.

"It's time to head to bed or Rudolph will skip our rooftop," Mom said, coaxing them up the steps.

Soon the horses were munching on hay, Pumba and Jazzie were curled up in their sheds, the hens were settled in their hutch, and Levi and Stetson were snuggled up on the porch.

Mom finished wrapping the last of the presents and stoked the fire while the new white calf snoozed by the Christmas tree.

All was quiet and peaceful on the farm.

That night, through the wind and the snow, Santa made his way to the old farmhouse on top of the hill.

Smoke rolled out of the chimney while the family stayed nestled in their beds. Santa quietly proceeded to his deliveries.

As he walked past the fireplace, he stopped and noticed there was still a stocking hung on the mantle with "Dad" stitched on it. With sadness in his heart, he finished placing beautifully wrapped packages under the tree.

He was heading back out into the snow when the white calf greeted him.

"Ho, Ho, Ho there, my little winter cow. Where did you come from?"

The little white cow nudged him and licked his mitten.

"You are a very special white calf, aren't you? You are going to bring strength, hope and joy to this family."

Santa pulled a carrot from the pocket of his red fur coat and fed it to the winter cow.

Patting him on his head, he hopped into his sleigh exclaiming, *"Merry Christmas!"*

A joyous Christmas morning came and the traditions continued as they had in years past, although, this year was a bit different.

Dad wasn't there to take a video of the boys running down the steps to the pile of presents under the tree. Nor could he help the boys build Legos, put their toy trucks together, or lean over and kiss Mom on the cheek with a loving smile. But family and relatives still gathered around the tree, opening presents and gratefully loving all that they had.

Then, unexpectedly the winter cow scrambled into the living room tripping over boxes and bows.

Laughing hysterically, the boys exclaimed, "What would Daddy do if he saw this white winter cow in our living room on Christmas morning?"

Every eye was open, glimmering and joyous. The stories began to flow and laughter filled the room.

They gathered around the table for Christmas dinner and "Winter" the cow was the highlight. Each child took turns feeding him and the love he returned to them was equally fulfilling.

Winter followed them around, imitating their every move, and the children's laughter was infectious.

5

Days, weeks, and months went by, and Winter grew quickly. His legs were strong and solid like that of a tree trunk. The broad shoulders that carried his stout neck gleamed white as he lifted his oxen head to "Mooo" for breakfast.

The rope-like tail that hung from his rear swung rapidly back and forth in excitement as Mom approached during morning feedings. A little rub on the forehead as she dumped his bucket of grain made his morning complete.

Scout, the miniature pony, tried to slide his nose in the bucket and grab a bite as Jazzie sneak attacked from the other side.

Winter's heart was so big, he didn't realize that his size alone could fight off his pasture mates. He just moved to the side and let them munch along with him.

Once his belly was full, he proceeded to lie down in a mound of hay and let the sunshine beat on his face.

Mom continued about her chores, mixing meals for all the equines that were lined up along the fence next to their buckets. Driving the big red tractor full of

hay out to the field, gathering dozens of eggs from the hen-house, and collecting fresh fruits and vegetables from the garden were all part of her daily routine.

A few hours later, as the sun neared the west side of the hill, Winter walked down to the edge of the pasture. Patiently waiting and peering to the end of the drive, he could hear the big yellow bus rumbling up the road. Then he spotted it, lifting his head high, he watched the boys scramble off the bus as they laughed and talked about their day.

From deep inside, Winter bellowed out his "HELLLOOOOOO" moo.

The boys looked up and squealed, "Hi, Winter!" Running up to the fence, they scratched the crown of his head and then took off toward the house.

Winter ducked his head, pounced his front feet down, kicked his heels up, and galloped back up the hill... sending Pumba, Jazzie, and Scout fleeing for their lives.

6

The daylight hours lessened and the colored leaves fell as the chilly air whistled through the woods. It would be a tough time of year for Winter's new family.

Out in the yard between the house and the woods, the boys were covered in dried leaves, playing a rugged game of football. Winter peered intently over the top fence rail, hoping they would include him in their game.

Suddenly the older boy stopped and gazed toward the wood-line. His neighbor friend, dressed in camouflage with a bow and arrow slung over his shoulder, was walking into the woods with his dad alongside him. The father's hand was on the neighbor boy's shoulder and it was obvious they were going over tactics for the evening hunt.

With football still in hand, the older boy stood frozen while the younger one followed his brother's gaze.

Wondering why the intense football game stopped, Winter mooed loudly and broke the boys' stare.

"Come on!" the younger boy said. "Let's go play with Winter. He's always good at lifting our spirits..."

Ducking his head and hiding his emotions, the older brother chucked the football and chased the younger boy up the hill to see Winter.

7

In the days following, the boys learned that when their soul felt a bit lonely, it was always a good idea to go interact with Winter. No matter what they did, the situation would end with entertainment and giggles.

The brothers didn't always feel their grief at the same time though. There were so many undetermined triggers. But when they did, they knew they had a place to go. Mom was always open to talk to them about Dad, but there was something about that white winter cow that brought them serenity.

There were also certain times, like one particular sunny warm day in November, when they just needed to be with him. So after arriving home from school and dumping their backpacks, they walked out to his field.

Winter lay there, sunbathing on top of the hill. With no words spoken, they laid down against him. He turned his nose to nudge them and then closed his eyes. The three of them lay there for a while, resting, relaxing, and thinking.

Now comfortable, the boys let their minds wander and dream of how they wanted to grow up and change the world... to bring back trust, communication and faithfulness to a world that seemed so big and untouchable. The warm embrace of the sun reminded them of the unconditional love that surrounded them.

After a while the younger boy decided to climb on Winter's back. Then the older boy climbed on as well.

Intrigued by their playfulness, Winter began to roll over... and the laughter began!

8

"Today is the day!" the younger boy squealed.

Mom walked into the kitchen and said, "I know, honey. It's Christmas Eve..."

"Nooo, Mom! It's Winter's birthday!" He was so excited he ran upstairs to wake his brother.

Shocked that her son had thought of Winter before Christmas, she decided to make the white cow a birthday surprise.

As the boys finished up their morning chores, Mom came outside with her creation.

Running to see what she had brought, they stopped at the bottom of the wooden porch steps. There she was, holding a double-layer carrot-topped, birthday "grain" cake!

The boys took turns slowly carrying the cake up the hill. They were thrilled to present their white winter cow—their four-legged friend, their best friend—his birthday "grain" cake.

Starting to argue over who was going to feed Winter the cake, the older boy said, "I am the oldest, I should do it!"

The younger boy's rebuttal was, "He loves me more, and I should do it!"

Pushing and shoving their way through the gate, the "grain" cake with carrots sticking out of the top, toppled out of both their arms and landed upside down in Winter's bucket!

With anger in his voice, the older boy said, "Look at what you did! You ruin everything. I don't need you. I don't need that stupid cow. I don't need anyone!" Then he spun around and stormed off down the hill toward the woods.

Looking down at the grain mush cake, with carrots now popping through the bottom, the younger boy couldn't believe what had just happened.

Winter, unaware of the boys' dispute, and so excited to have a sweet meal, shoved his snout in the middle of the mush and then used his tongue to sweep up the molasses frosting.

The younger boy stood there stoically, watching the winter cow eat his birthday cake as a tear slowly dripped down his cold cheek.

After all of the grain cake was sucked up, the boy turned and started walking slowly toward the wood-line with Winter at his heels.

9

Kicking rocks along the path to the woods, the younger boy started thinking about all his family had endured in the past few years.

He realized that with their emotional disappointment, his older brother felt helpless, powerless and alone. Failing to deliver the cake to the cow had created anger which made him defensive, declaring that he didn't need anyone.

But the younger brother knew that wasn't true. He also knew that holding your feelings inside and not expressing them was like a festering blister that would eventually pop.

And he knew his brother's blister had popped!

As the younger boy contemplated all of this, he noticed Winter had stopped at the edge of the tree-line which opened up to the trail to the river. The white cow paused to look at him and then proceeded to gallop down the trail toward the hill.

The boy hesitated and then called out for the white cow. Getting no response, he jogged down the path that Winter had chosen.

But soon, he was further from home than he was allowed to be, and he started to get nervous.

He followed Winter's tracks in the mud, but it was difficult because of all the other animal tracks on the trail.

There was a Y in the path ahead, and the young boy was unsure of which way to go. Then he spotted the white cow tracking down the left side.

Halfway down the narrow trail, the boy heard a loud *CRACK!* He and Winter stopped in their tracks.

A shriek of desperation came from the river's edge.

Three sets of legs began to gallop down the hill to the riverbank where they found the older boy stuck under a large tree branch.

Gasping for air, the older boy signaled for them with his hand.

Feeling helpless, and knowing he could not move the large tree limb, the younger brother fell to his knees and began praying for help.

Watching this, Winter walked over to the older boy and placed his square head against the side of the log. He pushed and pushed and pushed, until the massive tree branch rolled off the older boy's chest.

The younger boy ran to his brother, wrapped him in loving arms, and helped him to his feet.

"I'm s-s-sorry," the older brother began to say.

"Don't apologize to me, brother," the younger boy said. "We will always be here for each other. No matter what. And as long as we have faith and believe, then... *we are never alone!*"

The older brother smiled and said, "Remember how Dad always said, 'There is a Power greater than us... believe in it, believe in yourself, and stay true to both'? Well, believe me, little brother, I love you and together there is no mountain we can't climb!"

Winter then nuzzled in between them and nudged them toward home.

With very sore ribs, the older brother climbed onto the winter cow's back as the younger boy led the way home.

10

Once back in the warm farmhouse, the boys explained to Mom what happened that afternoon. She was so grateful that they were safely back home, and amazed at Winter's heroic efforts.

The boys stopped for a moment and the older one said, "You know, Mom... Winter is kind of like us. He's growing up without a dad but yet he still finds comfort in loyalty. Not only in us and our farm family, but by believing that as long as you have love and faith in your heart... there is no limit!"

Mom's heart was so full at that moment. She squeezed both boys tightly and said,

"Your father would be so proud of you. It doesn't matter what cards you are dealt in this life, it is how you play your hand that really counts!"

She kissed each of their foreheads and patted their butts up the stairs.

"Remember, it is Christmas Eve, so go to sleep before Santa comes!"

That evening as Santa arrived at the farm, he felt an overwhelming feeling of peace. He glanced over the roof and saw that special white winter Christmas cow nestled in the hay.

After dropping off his delivery, he stopped at Winter's stall. Pulling out a few carrots from his red coat pocket, he fed them to Winter and said, "I had a feeling that you would bring faith, hope and love to this family's future... and that is exactly what you have done!"

Santa gave the white cow a pat on the head and proceeded to his sleigh exclaiming, "Merry Christmas to all, and to all a good night!"

11

The next morning, the family joyously woke to Christmas with full, gracious and faithful hearts. With wrapping paper spread all over the family room, toys half put together on the kitchen floor, and Mom's eggs cooking on the stove, they heard a scratch at the door.

Mom and the boys looked at each other, then hesitantly went to the door while slowly opening it.

There, staring up at them, stood a scrawny, starved, long-haired black cat. He looked up at them with no energy left to meow, and just laid down.

The three of them looked at each other wondering... what this upcoming year was going to bring!

To be continued...

QUESTIONS FOR DISCUSSION

* ❖ Why do you think the author named the animals but not the boys?
* ❖ What names would you prefer? Why?
* ❖ What do you think happened to the dad? Why?
* ❖ Why do you think the author didn't mention why the father wasn't around?
* ❖ Do you think Winter is a good name for the cow? Why?
* ❖ What is the difference between a cow, a calf, a heifer, a steer and a bull?
* ❖ What do you think Winter really represented?
* ❖ Overall, what do you think the author was trying to portray?
* ❖ Do you think this is a true story? Why or why not?
* ❖ If you were to write a sequel to this story, what would it be about? Explain.

ABOUT THE AUTHOR

BECKY MATICIC has been an avid horseman since the age of ten. Growing up training horses, galloping at racetracks, and starting her own equine business over fifteen years ago, has given her not only vast insight to the nature of horses, but to the relationship they share with humans.

It was only after she became a widow with two young boys that she found out what was most important in life. She has since established a farm filled with animals—*New Leaf Acres* in Keymar, Maryland—in hope of inspiring and strengthening others.

Made in the USA
Middletown, DE
13 November 2020